Phil

Bill

Bill

Phil

Phil

Bill

Phil

Bill

Bill

Phil

Phil

Bill

Phil

Bill

Phil

Bill

Phil

Bill

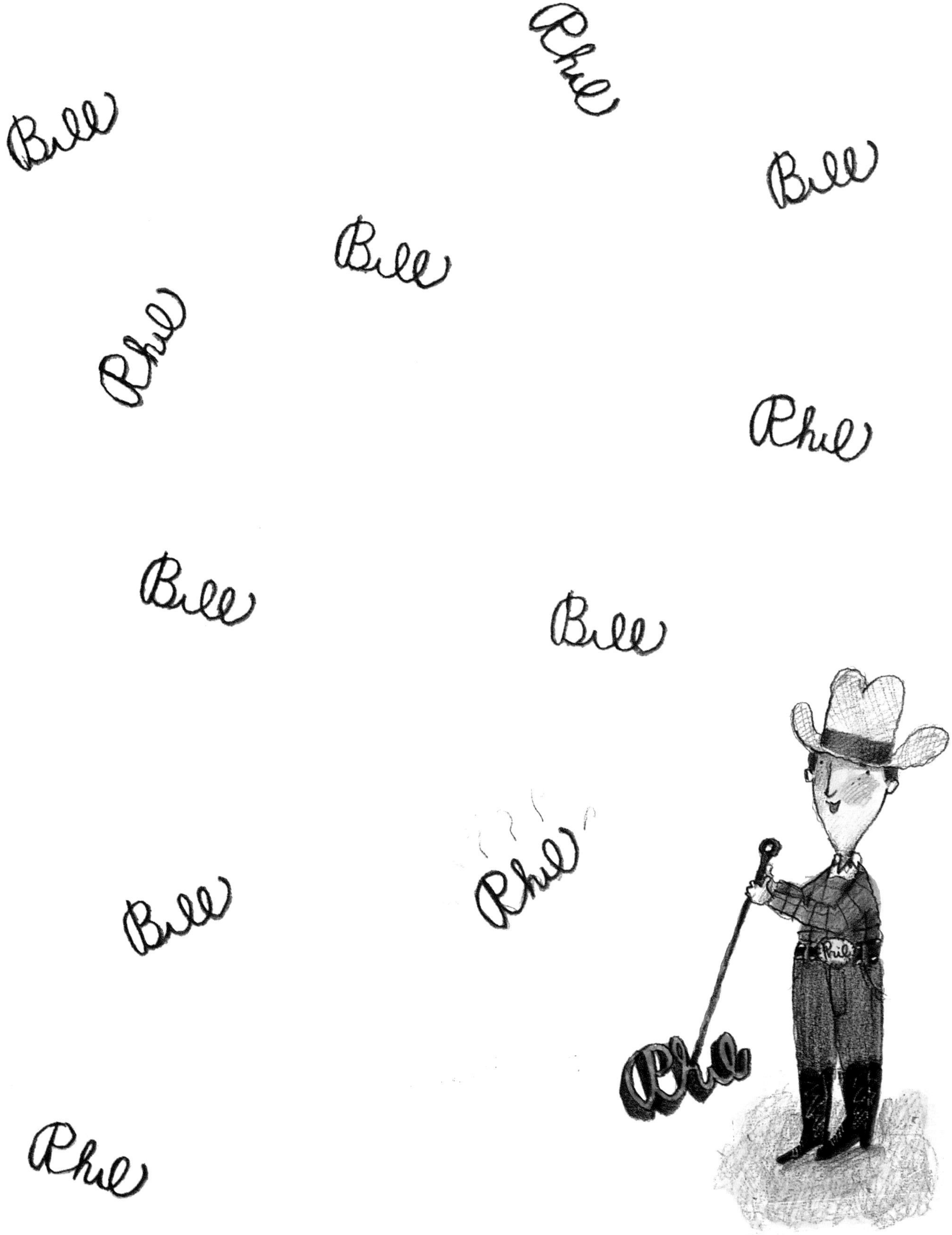
Phil
Bill
Bill
Bill
Phil
Phil
Bill
Bill
Bill
Phil
Phil
Phil

ON THE TRAIL WITH
MISS PACE

story by
Sharon Phillips Denslow

pictures by **G. Brian Karas**

Simon & Schuster Books for Young Readers

SIMON & SCHUSTER BOOKS FOR YOUNG READERS
An imprint of Simon & Schuster Children's Publishing Division
1230 Avenue of the Americas, New York, NY 10020
Text copyright © 1995 by Sharon Phillips Denslow
Illustrations copyright © 1995 by G. Brian Karas
All rights reserved including the right of reproduction in whole or in part in any form.
SIMON & SCHUSTER BOOKS FOR YOUNG READERS is a trademark of Simon & Schuster.
Designed by Christy Hale
The text of this book is set in Lubalin Graph
The illustrations are rendered in gouache, acrylic medium, pencil, charms,
twine, wildflowers, shrubs, and bandanna on a variety of papers.
Manufactured in the United States of America
10 9 8 7 6 5 4 3 2 1
Library of Congress Cataloging-in-Publication Data
Denslow, Sharon Phillips.
On the trail with Miss Pace / by Sharon Phillips Denslow ;
illustrations by G. Brian Karas.—1st ed., 1st American ed.
p.   cm.
Summary: Twins Bill and Phil spend an exciting vacation out west
at the same ranch as their teacher, Miss Pace, and
her boyfriend, the wild cowboy Last Bob.
ISBN 0-02-728688-6
(1. Teachers—Fiction.   2. Twins—Fiction.
3. West (U.S.)—Fiction.   4. Cowboys—Fiction.)
I. Karas, G. Brian, ill.   II. Title.
PZ7.D4330n   1995
(E)—dc20   94-38206

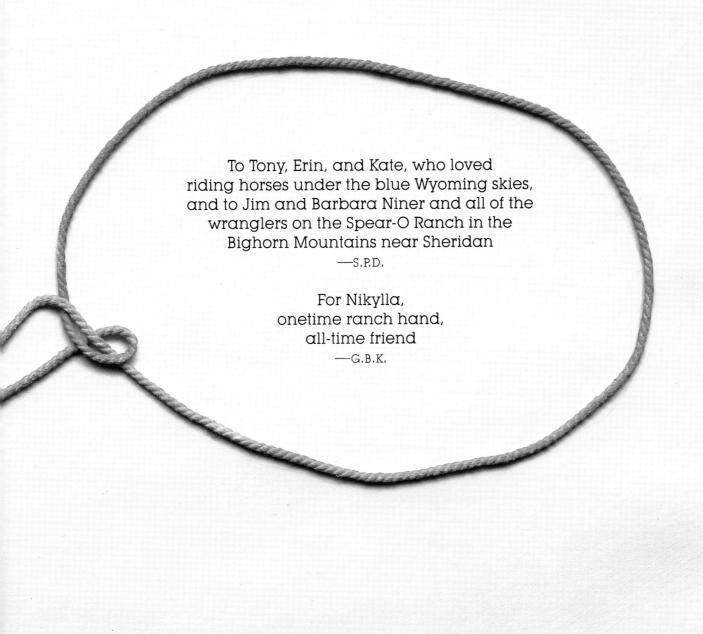

To Tony, Erin, and Kate, who loved
riding horses under the blue Wyoming skies,
and to Jim and Barbara Niner and all of the
wranglers on the Spear-O Ranch in the
Bighorn Mountains near Sheridan
—S.P.D.

For Nikylla,
onetime ranch hand,
all-time friend
—G.B.K.

A s soon as the final school bell of the year faded, Miss Pace put on her cowboy hat, her cowboy boots, and her belt with the mustang buckle. She climbed into her Jeep and roared off into the sunset.

"There's no place like the West," she said to the picture of the cowboy on her dashboard.

On Miss Penelope Bartlett's Ranch, there were no chalkboards, no pencil sharpeners, no papers to grade, and no school bells.

"Ahhhhh," Miss Pace said with satisfaction as she took a long, deep breath from the doorway of her cabin.

"What's she doing?" a voice whispered from the corner.

"Breathing, I reckon," an identical voice answered back.

"Don't let her see us yet!" the voice in the corner warned.

Miss Pace slowly opened her eyes, hoping for a mirage.

"Hey, Miss Pace!" the skinnier boy said, peeking out from behind the bed.

"Surprise!" the other twin yelled, tossing his cowboy hat into the air.

"Phil and Bill Trimble!" Miss Pace said. "What are you doing here?"

"We're on vacation, too," Phil said.

"We're here to keep you company," Bill added.

Miss Pace looked suspiciously at Phil and Bill.

"This isn't some kind of school trip I'm not aware of, is it? The whole class isn't hiding behind my cabin, are they?"

"Nope, there's just us." Phil and Bill beamed. "This is going to be a vacation you'll never forget."

Phil and Bill helped Miss Pace unload her gear from her Jeep. "Did you know that there's a real cowboy here on the Bearclaw Ranch?" Phil asked.

"There are several cowboys here," Miss Pace said.

"His name's Last Bob, and he rides a wild, one-eyed mustang called Handshaker," said Phil.

"Maybe he's just a story. We haven't seen him yet," said Bill.

"Last Bob is real," Miss Pace said. "He'll show up in his own good time."

"Wow, Miss Pace. Do you know him?" Phil asked.

"I do," Miss Pace said. "That's his photograph on the dashboard."

Phil and Bill dropped the bags in the dust and scrambled for the front seat of the Jeep.

"He's got a real cowboy hat with a snakeskin band!"

"That must be Handshaker's mane!"

"He could have stared down Billy the Kid!"

"He has blue eyes with gold flecks in them," Miss Pace said.

Both Phil and Bill turned to stare at Miss Pace, and then looked at each other and began to giggle.

"Miss Pace, are you sweet on Last Bob?"

"Miss Pace, are you going to marry Last Bob?"

Phil and Bill exchanged wild coyote calls. "Miss Pace and Last Bob sitting in a tree, k-i-s-s-i-n-g!" they sang.

Phil and Bill stuck to Miss Pace like clinging burrs for the rest of the day.

They followed her up to Waterfall Trail.

They followed her up to the Main House and watched while she had tea with Miss Penelope.

They followed her to the corral and watched her sketch the horses.

They saved a seat for her at supper.

"How thoughtful," Miss Pace murmured as she sat down.

Phil helped her butter her dinner rolls. Bill sweetened her tea. They both gave Miss Pace their small new potatoes with the skins on.

"We only eat mashed potatoes," Bill told her.

Suddenly a hush fell over the dining room.

"Look!" Phil said.

A tall cowboy with a mustache and blue eyes stood in the doorway.

"Last Bob!" Phil and Bill shouted.

"Where have you been?"

"We thought you were just a story!"

"Where's Handshaker?"

"Does he really have one eye?"

"Can we ride him sometime?"

"Well, boys," Last Bob said, "nobody's ever ridden Handshaker but me." He paused and looked down the table. "Of course, every year I do ask Miss Pace to ride Handshaker, but she never has."

Phil and Bill stared at Miss Pace.

"You two look like you could use some more grub,"
Last Bob said, dividing up his small new potatoes
with the skins on between Phil and Bill.
   "I only eat mashed potatoes," he whispered.

As soon as Miss Pace pulled on her boots the next morning, Phil and Bill were knocking on the door.

"Miss Pace, Last Bob says it's the perfect day for you to ride Handshaker."

"Handshaker is too tall," Miss Pace said, "and he only has one eye and gets skittish sometimes, and besides, no one except Last Bob has ever ridden him."

"But Last Bob invited you to ride Handshaker. You can do it, Miss Pace," Phil said.

"Come on, Miss Pace. Last Bob is waiting," Bill said.

Last Bob had four horses bridled by the fence.

"The boys tell me you're wanting to ride Handshaker."

"They do, do they?" Miss Pace said, staring hard at Phil and Bill.

"I'll help the boys with their saddles; then I'll help you with Handshaker."

"It's all right," Miss Pace said. "If I can ride him, surely I can saddle him." Handshaker swiveled his ears and looked at Miss Pace as she cinched up the saddle.

"Lead the way, Miss Pace!" Phil yelled.

Miss Pace gingerly turned Handshaker toward
the high meadow.

"What do you think of him?" Last Bob asked her.

"He's doing fine," Miss Pace said, relaxing a little.

"You should ride him in a canter," Last Bob said.
"He's as smooth as a frog's underside."

"Yeah, let's canter!" Phil and Bill yelled.

Before Miss Pace quite knew what had happened,
they were all cantering across the mountain meadow
under the blue western sky.

Handshaker was very smooth, but he was also very fast. He and Miss Pace raced ahead of the others.

Miss Pace laughed and waved her hat. "Hurry up, slowpokes."

Quickly Miss Pace dropped her hand and grabbed the saddle horn. Something was wrong. Somehow the saddle was moving.

"Whoa!" Miss Pace shouted. "Whoa!"

Miss Pace was no longer sitting upright on the horse's back! She was leaning off to the side like the arm of a giant cactus!

Miss Pace flung herself to the ground and sat up in time to see Handshaker disappear up the trail, his reins flying and the saddle hanging upside down under his stomach.

"You belly bloater!" she yelled. "You rascal! Come back here!"

Last Bob jumped off his horse and rushed up to Miss Pace.

"Are you all right?" he asked, smoothing her hair.

"Just dusty," Miss Pace said. "Go on after my horse!"

Last Bob grinned and took off.

"Wait till everyone hears about this!"
Bill said, his mouth and eyes both widened
into great, amazed circles.

Miss Pace groaned.

"You were like a stuntman," Phil said, "the way
you jumped off. And did you see the way Last Bob
rushed up to you?"

"He thinks you're brave," Bill said.

That night Miss Pace lay awake for a long time.
Last Bob and Phil and Bill had told everyone on the
Bearclaw about Handshaker and her, so she'd
spent the evening telling the story over and over.
It was good to be in her nice, quiet cabin.

"Is she still up?" a familiar voice whispered.
"'Course not. Her lights are all turned out."
"Well, wake her up. Last Bob said to get her up."
"Phil and Bill, what are you whispering about outside my door?"
"Miss Pace! Hurry! Come and see! Hurry!"

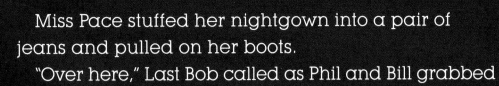

Miss Pace stuffed her nightgown into a pair of
jeans and pulled on her boots.
   "Over here," Last Bob called as Phil and Bill grabbed
Miss Pace's hands, steering her out the door.
   "Look!"

Miss Pace looked. Streaming across the sky in glimmering bands of green and violet and blue and pink and yellow, the northern lights danced.

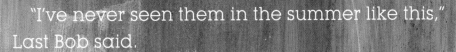

"I've never seen them in the summer like this,"
Last Bob said.

"We've never seen them at all!" Phil and Bill
said together.

"Once, when I was a girl . . ." Miss Pace began.
Then she turned to the boys. "Quick, go wake
everybody! No one should miss the glorious borealis
over the Bearclaw!"

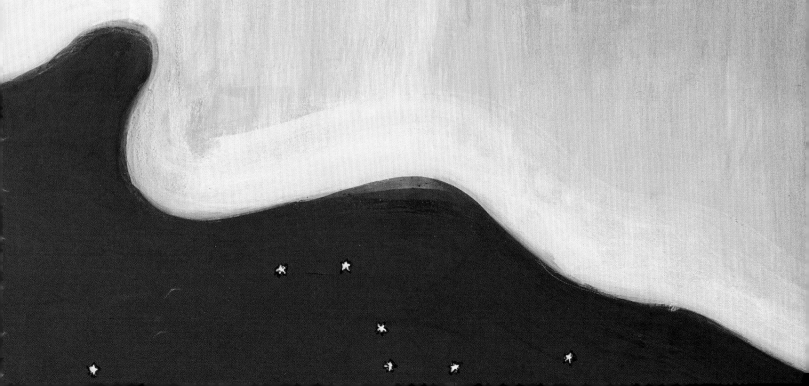

Miss Pace smiled at Last Bob
as Phil and Bill hurried away. "There's
no place like the West," she said.
    "Nope," Last Bob said, reaching
for her hand and smiling back at her
through his grizzled mustache.
    "Wow!" Bill shouted from somewhere
behind them. "It's just like the movies!"

Phil Bill Phil Phil

Bill Phil Phil

Bill

Phil Bill

Bill Phil

Bill Phil

Bill Phil

Phil Bill Bill

Phil Bill Phil Phil